THE TOYMAKER'S LOAVES

written by Jennifer Zabel

illustrated by Christopher Masters

FREDERICK WARNE
LONDON

About The Author

Jennifer Zabel was born in 1947 in Bradford, Yorkshire. She attended Bradford Girls' Grammar School and the University of Bradford. As part of her honours degree course in French and Russian, she chose to make a study of prize-winning French and Soviet children's literature. She has always taken delight in writing children's stories and hopes to make this her career. She has spent a considerable part of the last ten years living abroad— Czechoslovakia, France, Canada and Belgium—and she is now living in Marlow, Buckinghamshire. She is married with two young sons.

About The Artist

Christopher Masters was born in Watford in 1944. He was educated at Watford Grammar School where he specialized in the sciences (although his own wish was to study art). A self-taught cartoonist and illustrator in his spare time, he works at the Lister Institute of Preventive Medicine at Elstree as a medical technician. He lives at Oxhey, Watford.

First published by Frederick Warne (Publishers) Ltd, London, England 1977
ISBN 0 7232 2046 8

© Frederick Warne & Co. Ltd 1977

Printed in Great Britain by William Clowes & Sons Ltd, London, Beccles and Colchester

2580.577

Mr Pinkerman was a toymaker. He carved his toys out of wood. He and his little dog Butterball worked very hard making wooden engines, wooden dolls, wooden forts, wooden bears, in fact they made every wooden toy imaginable.

As each one was finished it was put on the shelf—for the window was already full—and there it stayed.

Nobody bought Mr Pinkerman's toys any more.

People said they were too expensive. They preferred to buy their children cheaper toys made of brightly coloured plastic and metal which were sold in smart new shops gleaming with paint and sparkling with glass.

One of these shops had just opened opposite Mr Pinkerman's premises. It was the first thing he saw every morning when he drew back the curtains. It made him so bad tempered that it quite spoilt his breakfast.

The last straw came when he visited the timberyard.
He had only enough money to buy
the smallest piece of wood.
It was scarcely enough
to make a couple
of bricks!

'My days as a toymaker are over,' he decided sadly as he rode home on the top of a bus with a bag of currant buns to cheer himself up. 'I must find myself a new job. Perhaps I could drive a bus . . . or be a bus conductor . . . or . . .' He bit into a bun to help himself think. 'I know! I'll be a baker!'

It seemed such a good idea that he couldn't imagine why he hadn't thought of it before—he had always had a sweet tooth. Mr Pinkerman beamed and offered a bun to the bus conductor.

As soon as he got home he set to work.
First of all he packed up his unsold toys
in a huge box and hauled them up the wobbly
ladder into the loft to live with the spiders.

Then workmen came to fit an enormous oven in the work-
room, rows of trays in the window, and a brand new counter
in the shop.

Finally, with a big lump in his throat—Mr Pinkerman had been a toymaker a long time—he took down the sign PINKER-MAN TOYS and hammered up another which said . . .

BUTTERBALL BAKERY

(Butterball felt very proud.)

Before he began to bake Mr Pinkerman thought it would be advisable to look at some cookery books, so he and Butterball took a trip to the library. He came away with a pile so high he could hardly see over them.

While Butterball had been hunting for recipes for dog biscuits he had discovered a marvellous book all about dinosaurs which he just had to take too. His mouth watered at the thought of those huge bones!

Mr Pinkerman's first batch of bread was a disaster! The dough wouldn't rise and the loaves were so flat that Butterball thought they were meant to be pancakes and rushed for the treacle tin.

He upset it all over himself.

Mr Pinkerman had to stop work to give him a bath, and it was not until he had his arms deep in suds that he remembered three chocolate cakes and a tray of mince pies which were waiting to come out of the oven.

When they finally appeared they were burnt to a cinder!

But Mr Pinkerman was a patient man and after a few more attempts he produced a perfect loaf, so round and brown, and smelling so warmly delicious that they wanted to eat it themselves.

They had it for tea, oozing with thick golden butter.

Now it was time to start baking for the customers. On opening day Mr Pinkerman got up at four o'clock in the morning to make the first batch of bread. He shaped the dough into balls, while Butterball kept watch over the loaves in the oven.

As soon as they had turned just the right shade of golden brown, Butterball would give a bark to warn Mr Pinkerman it was time to take them out. Butterball was determined there would be no more burnt offerings!

By nine o'clock the last bun had been sugared, the last cake had been iced, and Mr Pinkerman turned the sign on the door to OPEN.

WOOF!

But lunchtime came and went and nobody had been in to buy as much as a plain bread roll. 'Monday is always a bad day for sales,' said Mr Pinkerman bravely. 'People always buy too much food at the weekend.'

Butterball took his nose out of his dinosaur book to put a comforting paw on Mr Pinkerman's knee.

During the whole of that day they had only one customer. His name was Cuthbert, and he often used to come into Mr Pinkerman's shop to look at the toys.

'My mum wants a loaf of bread, but she told me not to buy it here,' he confessed. 'My mum says toymakers can't bake bread the way real bakers can!'

'But I *am* a real baker now,' said Mr Pinkerman. 'Try a bun and see if it isn't true.' Then he thought of all the cakes and bread and buns that would go to waste if they weren't eaten soon. 'Let's have a party,' he suggested. 'Bring all your friends—there's plenty to eat . . .'

The party was a huge success. The piles of food disappeared like magic. 'My baking can't be that bad,' muttered Mr Pinkerman ruefully.

'And there was nothing wrong
with my toymaking either!'
he shouted. 'Follow me.'

He led the overfed but happy band of children back to his shop and up the wobbly ladder to the loft, where they were allowed to choose a toy to take home. Mr Pinkerman suddenly felt quite happy as he watched his delighted guests trooping home in the moonlight.

But the next day Mr Pinkerman and Butterball weren't feeling at all happy. Still no customers came into the shop and they had eaten so many buns and cakes that they were feeling really sick and extremely sorry for themselves.

Tucked up in bed that night, Mr Pinkerman reviewed the situation. 'If people still think of me as a toymaker they will never buy my bread, so they will never discover what a good baker I am. But perhaps I am still a toymaker at heart,' he sighed. 'I must admit that it is much more exciting to make a toy engine than a dull loaf of bread . . .'

There was a long silence.

Suddenly on went the light. 'I've got it! I've got it!' Mr Pinkerman cried, bouncing up and down in his bed. 'If I can't make wooden toys I'll make bread toys—out of dough!'

Sleep was now quite out of the question so down they went to
the kitchen to start work on the new loaves.

They worked all night, and when dawn came they collapsed
in a tired heap to wait for opening time.

Imagine the amazement of the passers-by when they saw Butterball Bakery's window display that day! Piled high on the shelves were fat little teddybears, chubby dolls, marvellous motor cars and beaming golliwogs, all with the golden crustiness of fresh bread.

There were iced-cake forts and fairy castles, buns the shape of swans, marzipan bricks and jam tarts with clown faces.

All day long the children pressed their noses against the window in ecstasy while Mr Pinkerman busily wrapped loaves and packed pastries for their mothers. One of his first customers had been Cuthbert's mother. 'Some teddybear bread and six marzipan bricks, please. That loaf my Cuthbert bought here the other day was delicious, Mr Pinkerman. I always knew you'd do well!'

Mr Pinkerman and Butterball exchanged a sly wink.

By five o'clock there were only a few crumbs to be seen. 'Oh, dear! Oh, dear!' groaned Mr Pinkerman. 'We have sold every loaf in the shop!' Butterball looked up at him in amazement. Surely he didn't regret their wonderful day?

'I forgot to save a loaf for us,' Mr Pinkerman explained. I will have to go out and *buy* one!'

Then he began to laugh. He laughed and he laughed until the tears ran down his cheeks and his sides ached.

The toymaker's loaves were going to be a great success!